BLITZ RUMS HUIII!

FLASH BANG WHEEE!

by Karen Clark

illustrated by Ian White

mantra

Amber war ein kleines Mädchen, und sie
wohnte in London, in einem kleinen Haus.

Amber was a little girl who lived in a little house in London.

Eines Nachts guckte Amber aus ihrem
Schlafzimmerfenster, als sie plötzlich etwas am
Himmel geschah: BLITZ, RUMS, HUIII!

One night Amber was staring out of her bedroom window,
when all of a sudden there was a FLASH, BANG and a WHEEE
coming from the sky!

Amber kriegte Angst, und sie rannte zu ihrer Mama und sagte: "Mami, Mami, was ist denn DAS für ein Krach?"

Ihre Mama erklärte ihr, dass dieser Krach, den sie da hörte, von einem Feuerwerk kommt.

"Was ist ein Feuerwerk, Mami?"

"Komm und guck' es dir an," sagte die Mama.

Amber was frightened and she ran to her Mum saying, "Mum, Mum, what IS that noise?"
Her Mum explained that the noises she could hear were fireworks.
"What are fireworks Mum?"
"Come and see," said Mum.

Sie gingen ans Schlafzimmerfenster und schauten hinaus.
BLITZ, RUMS, HUIII!
Der ganze Himmel war voll glitzernder Sterne und bunter Farben.
Amber hatte immer noch ein klein bisschen Angst und klammerte sich
fest an ihre Mama.

They went to the bedroom window and watched.
FLASH, BANG, WHEEE!
The whole sky was full of glittery stars and beautiful colours.
Amber was still a little bit scared and held on to her Mum tightly.

"Morgen Abend wenn es dunkel wird," sagte ihre Mama, "gehen wir mit Papa in den Park und schauen uns das Feuerwerk an. Es ist sehr hübsch, auch wenn es manchmal großen Krach macht."

"Tomorrow night when it is dark," said Mum, "we'll go to the park with Dad and watch some fireworks. They are very pretty even though they sometimes make loud noises."

Am nächsten Abend zog sich die ganze Familie Mützen, Mäntel und Schals an und wanderte zum Park. Es war sehr, sehr dunkel. Amber war noch nie nachts im Park gewesen.

The next night the whole family got all dressed up in hats, coats and scarves and walked to the park. It was very, very dark. Amber had never been to the park at night before.

Im Park waren viele Leute und viele Kinder liefen herum. Amber saß bei ihrem Papa auf den Schultern. Sie sah ein großes Feuer mit orangefarbigen Flammen, die in den Himmel sprühten.

There were lots of people in the park and lots of children running around. Amber's Dad carried her on his shoulders. She could see a big bonfire with orange flames leaping to the sky.

Plötzlich: BLITZ, RUMS, HUIII!
Der ganze Himmel war voll glitzernder Sterne und bunter Farben.
Amber versuchte tapfer zu sein, aber die lauten Kracher erschreckten
sie, und sie bekam doch ein bisschen Angst. Da entdeckte sie ihren
Freund Jamie mit seinem Papa.

Suddenly, FLASH, BANG, WHEEE!
The sky was full of glittery stars and beautiful colours. Amber was trying to be brave but the loud noises made her jump and she was starting to feel a bit frightened. Then she saw her friend Jamie with his Dad.

"Oooh!" rief Jamie. "Guck' mal DER da, Amber!"
Als Amber sah, wie Jamie sich über das Feuerwerk freute, hatte sie schon sehr viel weniger Angst.

Jedes Mal, wenn es besonders laut rumste, hüpften sie beide in die Luft.
Es machte den beiden riesigen Spaß, aber schließlich war das Feuerwerk zu Ende.
"Nun kommt, ihr zwei," sagte Papa, "es ist Zeit nach Hause zu gehen."

"Oooh!" shouted Jamie. "Look at THAT one, Amber!"
When Amber saw how much Jamie was enjoying the fireworks, she didn't feel quite so scared anymore.

Every time there was a loud bang, they both jumped up and down.
They were having a really exciting time when the fireworks ended.
"Come on you two," Dad said, "it's time to go home."

Amber war so müde, dass sie schon einschlief, während sie noch auf Papas Schultern saß.

Amber was so tired that she fell asleep riding on her Dad's shoulders.

HINWEISE FÜR ELTERN UND ERZIEHER

Diese Geschichte wurde geschrieben, um kleinen Kindern dabei zu helfen, ihre Ängste zu überwinden.

Wenn man einem Kind eine Geschichte über ein bevorstehendes Ereignis erzählt, ist es besser darauf vorbereitet.

In BLITZ, RUMS, HUIII! verliert das kleine Mädchen langsam ihre Angst, als sie ihren Freund entdeckt, dem das Feuerwerk und die Kracher, die sie so erschreckten, Spaß machen.

REGELN ZUM UMGANG MIT FEUERWERKSKÖRPERN

* Feuerwerkskörper in einem Behälter mit festem Deckel aufbewahren
* Immer nur einen Feuerwerkskörper herausnehmen und den Deckel sofort wieder schließen
* Feuerwerkskörper NIEMALS in die Tasche stecken
* Hinweise mit Hilfe einer Taschenlampe oder Handlampe sorgfältig durchlesen, dabei NIEMALS offenes Feuer verwenden
* Feuerwerkskörper auf Armeslänge mit einer langen Kerze oder einem extra langen Streichholz anzünden
* Weit zurück gehen und sich NIEMALS einem angezündeten Feuerwerkskörper wieder nähern, er könnte Ihnen ins Gesicht explodieren
* Alle Kinder müssen beim Feuerwerk gut beaufsichtigt werden
* Feuerwerkskörper niemals werfen
* Alle Haustiere und anderen Tiere einsperren
* Vorsicht bei Wunderkerzen, sie sollten nur mit Handschuhen angefasst werden. Wunderkerzen in einem Wassereimer löschen, sowie sie ausgebrannt sind

GUIDANCE NOTES FOR PARENTS AND CARERS

The aim of this story is to help small children overcome their fears.
Telling a story about an event can often prepare a child for a new experience.
In FLASH, BANG, WHEEE! the little girl's fears are abated when she sees her
friend enjoying both the fireworks and the noises coming from them.

FIREWORKS CODE
* Keep fireworks in a sealed box or tin
* Use them one at a time, replacing the lid immediately
* NEVER put fireworks in your pocket
* Read the instructions carefully using a torch or hand lamp.
  NEVER use a naked flame
* Light fireworks at arm's length using a taper or a firework lighter
* Stand well back and NEVER return to a firework after it has been lit.
  It could explode in your face.
* Ensure that all children with fireworks are well supervised
* Never throw fireworks
* Keep all pets and animals indoors
* Take care with sparklers, wear gloves to hold them.
  Dispose of sparklers in a bucket of water as soon as they are finished

To Amber, Andy & my mum for help and inspiration
K.C.

For Helena & Archie
I.W.

MANTRA
5 Alexandra Grove, London N12 8NU
www.mantrapublishing.com